Kimako's Story

Kimako's Story

BY JUNE JORDAN

Illustrated by Kay Burford

Houghton Mifflin Company Boston

Text Copyright © 1981 by June Jordan
Illustrations copyright © 1981 by Kay Burford

Printed in the United States of America
BP 10 9 8 7 6 5 4 3 2

Library of Congress Cataloging in Publication Data
Jordan, June, 1936-
    Kimako's Story.

    Summary: A little girl describes her life in the
city where she works poetry puzzles indoors and has
outdoor adventures with the dog that she is taking
care of for a friend.
    [1. City and town life—Fiction.   2. Dogs—Fiction]
I. Burford, Kay.   II. Title.
PZ7.J763Ki   [E]   81-2894
ISBN 0-395-31604-9   AACR2
PAP ISBN 0-395-60338-2

Dedicated to
REBECCA WALKER LEVENTHAL
and to
Little Valerie on West 20th Street
in Manhattan, New York.

My name is Kimako. I am seven going on
eight. This is the best way I always like to
sit.

On the bottom step of the stoop and in
front of my mother I can see everything
and everybody. Not only that: I can stay up

as late as nine or ten o'clock, outside. And
not only that: When my mother makes me
sit this way, then nobody bothers me. Not
even Roderico who is ten and who is crazy
because all the time he wants to beat up on
me or my cousin, Valerie. I mean, like some

other boys they would say, "Hi" or "Where you going?" But Roderico! He will just come over to you and punch you one.

My mother makes me sit on the stoop when she brushes and oils and combs and braids my hair into corn rows. Corn rows take a long while to do. If people talk to my mother a lot or if my Baby Brother, Charlie, is cranky in the carriage a lot, then the corn rows can take as long as two hours.

I have thick hair and my mother says I am "tender-headed." What she means is that sometimes a friend of hers will tell my mother a story that makes her laugh so hard until she forgets and pulls the comb through my hair too fast and that can really hurt!

Or sometimes my mother is in a hurry to finish my hair because it's so late and so she starts brushing and combing very fast. She yanks my head around a little bit. I say, "Ow." And she says, "What?! You tender-headed?"

Anyway it doesn't hurt most of the time.
And so I like my mother to do my hair.

We sit on the street, and I am safe. If my
mother stops combing my hair for a minute
so we can eat ice cream cones, then I can
lean my elbow on her knee and feel how
much I will have to grow before my
mother's knee will be like a table that is just
the right height for me.

Before this year I used to sit on the stoop,
and my mother used to comb my hair into
corn rows almost every day.

But now it's different. Tonight is special.
It's because this is a holiday. That's why
she's hanging out with me and Charlie, the
way we used to do.

My mother had to stop because she had to go to work. When she comes home after work she likes to stay in the house. Working makes her tired. So she changed my hair to an Afro. She taught me how to keep the Afro full and looking nice, by myself. She said the Afro would save time. Maybe it does.

But I miss the corn rows on the top of my head. And I miss being out on the street for hours right between the knees of my mother, safe from Roderico and safe from going to bed too early to fall asleep.

When my mother began to work she said I would have to stay off the streets until she came home. Then when she came home she said I could only go outside long enough to run to the grocery store on the corner, and then back again.

FRESH FRUIT AND VEGETABLES

The house is okay, but I hate it. What can you do in the house?

We live in an apartment that has windows looking out on other apartments and other windows. You can't see the street. You can't see any one of the four trees on the block. You can hear but you can't see the heavy A & P trucks as they crash around trying to back into the parking lot behind the supermarket.

You can't see the mailman taking a break with a can of beer on the stoop next to mine. You can't see Bobby and his girlfriend, Virginia, listening to disco on the portable radio, and you can't see them practice dancing together. You can't see Bobby at all. Bobby is about seventeen years old and very cute and he always asks me when I'm growing up enough so he can marry me.

Virginia thinks he's being corny when he does that. But I don't mind anything he says to me.

You can't see Theresa walking back from Eighth Avenue where she buys three or four candy bars at a trip, every afternoon, because her mother's boyfriend gives her so much money. Theresa is going to be fat and have bad teeth if she eats all of that candy. If I could see her coming, then she could give me some of the candy and not get fat so fast. But I can't. I can't see her or her candy from inside the house.

What you can do inside is watch TV. But even my Baby Brother, Charlie, knows that watching TV is like walking on two legs. I mean, so what? TV seems like potato chips to me. If you chew up a few, if you eat a whole one or two bags of potato chips by yourself, it doesn't help. After you eat them you still feel hungry and, besides, after that, you need to drink something, fast. But I don't mind TV if there are a lot of people talking loud, and not listening to each other, in the house, at the same time.

One more thing you can do in the house is read, or write. My cousin, Sekou, goes to City College, and then he brings me by a book to read sometimes and sometimes I like doing that. A book he gave me is about poetry. I like it the best of all, and because you have to figure out the words, it's better to be inside the house.

These are some of the poetry puzzles I have. They start out easy, and then they get to be harder and more interesting to me. I like to copy the puzzles on my own piece of paper where I can work on them but not be messing up my book!

Poem Puzzle No. 1:

Roses are red
Violets are blue
Roll out of _____
And lace up a _____
Butter the _____
But try something _____

Poem Puzzle No. *2:*

This is a wall in my _____
That I can pretty well clean with a _____
And a _____
Then I _____ Whatever I _____
Or I tear downstairs to ride on my _____

Poem Puzzle No. *3:*

If somebody don't know how to jump _____
He must be lazy or must be a _____

15

Poem Puzzle No. 4:

When it rains I see
Things looking really clear and very
Soft to me
When the _____ comes out
All I have to do is _____ and _____
And _____

Poem Puzzle No. 5:

I want to cross every street
In the world and never come back
I want to _____
Red and yellow _____ and _____

Poem Puzzle No. 6:

I'm gonna be smart I'm gonna be strong
I'd like _____
I'd like to be rich I'd like to be free
I'd like _____

Poem Puzzle No. 7:

How it feels when everything's dark
I say how it feels with everything dark
My mother thinks I'm stretched out sleeping
But if I can I _____
And then I _____
And then I _____

But I was telling you about my mother
and the stoop on the street. I was telling
you how she says "no" and she says I "can't
go," nowhere, but I do have a plan.

Remember Bobby who is seventeen? Well, Bobby found this raggedy dog that was dying for food and that didn't have no water, neither. But Bobby took the puppy home and it grew into a big old Airedale that likes to knock you down just jumping up to kiss you on the face. His name is *Bucks* because Bobby teases all the time about how you could buy his dog for a couple of bucks: You could just up and take him away for two or three dollars.

Anyhow, Bucks got so big and Bucks
stayed so playful until Bobby had to train
him some to act right and not to pull so
hard on the leash and how to be choosy
about who to kiss and how to kiss people
without laying them flat out on the sidewalk.

I heard about the whole thing from Theresa
who is still, everyday, eating a bunch of
candy bars by her selfish fat self, up and
down the block.

Then Bobby had to go to Puerto Rico for

a wedding in the family and he asked my
mother could his Little Girlfriend (meaning
me) take care of Bucks for a week. I knew
that was going to mean walking Bucks outside three or four or five times a day, and at
night, and do you know what? My mother
asked Bobby if Bucks would bite me or
Charlie.

Bobby said, "Positively *no*."

My mother asked Bobby if Bucks would
protect me and Charlie from crazy folks like
Roderico and the drunks on Eighth Avenue.

Bobby said, "Definitely *yes*."

So my mother told Bobby it was okay
about Bucks!

You see that window up there? That's
where I used to have to hang around,
dumb, because I couldn't see a thing!

But then! For the whole week I got to
take care of Bucks this was me: Follow the
dots around the neighborhood! That was me
and Bucks: *Outside the house!*

- PARK -

MET
x THERESA
HERE

TREE

WE PASSED
x RODERICO
HERE

x
WHERE WE
SAW BOY
WITH LONG ARM

TREE

STEPS
WHERE I
X SIT WITH
MY MOTHER

MILTON'S
x

BEST
BUCK'S
HYDRANT
x

GROCERY
STORE
X

THE LADY
STOOD HERE
x

I know I told you I have a plan, and I do! And I'm getting to it. But first I have to remember not to forget about that one week with Bucks because that was about my favorite week since the one when school let out.

What happened was we went everywhere together, and because Bucks is Best Dog I was safe on the streets, again. Nobody bothered me a bit.

I felt like I was on a vacation. I felt like I could have been sick with measles because all of a sudden I was out of the house, and the sky looked so bright and the traffic and the strangers and the kids around where I live all looked to me so much the same and so different and so exciting until I didn't say anything mean to anybody, not even to Roderico, until Bobby came back!

On Eighth Avenue there was this store I used to like to stand around and watch before my mother had to go to work. This was the store:

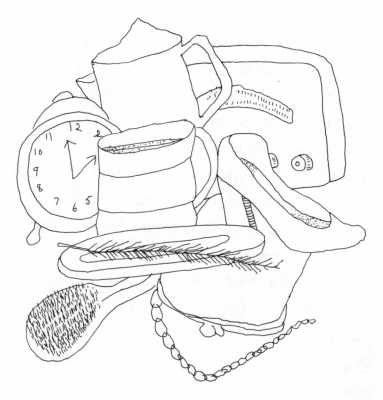

I was very interested in the *cash* part of it.
And I used to try and check out the ugly junk
that was piled into outdoor boxes. I wanted to
figure out if anything my mother kept in our
apartment was "Antique" or "Old Things" that
Milton would trade me for cash.

But you know how sooner or later there
always comes along a grownup can't keep her

nose out your business. So one afternoon I'm checking through the junk with Bucks sitting down nice as can be, at the end of the leash, when this lady shows up like Christopher Columbus looking straight at America, only she is looking straight at me and just have to ask me my name and if I can read and do I know about the tacky-looking books Milton is selling for ten cents apiece.

I say something like, "Yes, Ma'am," you know, being polite in case she's a teacher I

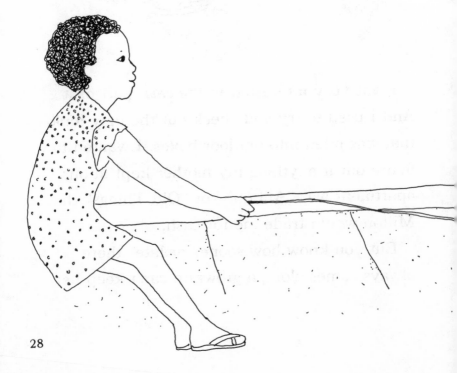

will run into, or something. But she can't let things alone, so she puts her arm around my shoulders (and Bucks begins this low growling sound), and she reads off the titles, aloud, like she's reading to I don't know to what! *"The Helen Keller Story, The Jackie Robinson Story, The Jungle Books,"* she says. And then this lady says she wants to buy me "the books of your choice!" And I'm standing there, tongue-tied, because I figure if she gives me three dimes instead, I can buy some candy of my own and catch up with Theresa, once and for all. But Bucks, who is Best Dog, jerks up from his spot, and now he's heading himself and me, both, over to the nearby hydrant, which he wants to use, right away.

So Bucks saved me.

The next morning, two blocks down, I saw this boy with an arm must have been fifteen feet long. He was wearing a huge, thick cardboard sleeve around his arm, and he was running around with the long arm waving around in the air like a flagpole coming out of his shoulder. Well, seeing that was worth the fact that, first off, I was sure I must have walked into the wrong neighborhood, by mistake, because I never saw a boy with an arm like that before that day, and even Bucks bounced backwards once he got a good look at the thing.

But the most fun was the park. The park was three short and four long blocks away from my street, and so my mother would never let me go that far unless she, or my cousin, Sekou, or somebody else who was really old, was to almost carry me there, like I was Charlie in a baby carriage.

The park was full of trees and bushes and dogs and men who wore the same shirt and the same pants, and no socks, day after day, while they played checkers on the concrete tables or they passed around brown paper bags of wine and whiskey. That was one end of the park.

At the other end there was a wading pool
for children like me. The water kept spraying
fresh out of the mouths of two sea lions made
out of cement. It was pretty nice and the
water was cool.

But Bucks bounced right into the middle of the pool and scared away everybody — the men and the other kids — because he raced around, dripping wet and shaking himself dry as soon as he got close to somebody's leg. Bucks thought he was having a bath, and so he kept racing around like that and then back, splashing high into the pool, and then out again, chasing the other people who were screaming and laughing and running away from him!

After a little while, Bucks and I were the only ones in the whole park. That was beautiful.

One morning, on Bucks's first walk for the day, it was raining hard. We went over to the park to look at everything, and do you know what we found?

Inside the concrete monkey jungle there was a regular man, a real man, squeezed up into one of the holes! The man was fast asleep. He must have been there all night long. Bucks and I stood there a minute, to see if he would snore or wake up, but he didn't, so we left him alone.

That afternoon, after the rain stopped, Bucks and I went back to the park looking for the man in the hole. But he was gone. But now we saw maybe nine or ten of the men who always drink or play at the concrete tables or who like to lie down on the benches, face up to the trees, and one of them was holding a gigantic watermelon. And another man took out this switchblade and he cut the watermelon into little pieces that the first man handed around to everyone. There were even seconds on that watermelon. And the first man gave me a piece too, and I said, "Thank you," but I didn't eat it because my mother would kill me if she heard I put anything that a stranger gave me into my mouth. But I thought that was really something, that watermelon, and the ten men in the park.

Now it's time for the plan. I know! So
Bobby came back from Puerto Rico and
Bucks went with him, away. But I never
stopped loving Bucks. And I never forgot the

way the two of us did everything, or what we did. And this is my plan. When my mother asks me what do I want for my birthday, which is coming up in August (I'm a Leo), I am going to tell her I want a little Bucks. I want to find a puppy that will grow up the way Bucks grew. But I'll call my dog *Buck,* for short.

And, if she says okay then I'll be back outside again! And if she says no, then I'm not sure what I'll do. But you know I will figure out something.

Anyway, and this is the very last poetry puzzle I can let you have for now:

Please wish me nothing but _____
So I can _____ with Buck!

Thanks a lot,

Kimako Anderson
New York City